RUDY AND JOEY

Ordinary Children in an Extraordinary Time

JOE POWERS

Copyright © 2017 Joe Powers
All rights reserved
First Edition

Fulton Books, Inc.
Meadville, PA

First originally published by Fulton Books 2017

ISBN 978-1-63338-501-6 (Paperback)
ISBN 978-1-63338-502-3 (Digital)

Printed in the United States of America

JOEY GREX

He looked over the cemetery and found what he was looking for—the marker with the name Ben Joey Grex, November 3, 1955, to December 24, 1973. It was still hard for him to fathom. A waste? According to whom you asked, I guess. Still, it was apparent that whether or not you considered it a waste, Joey Grex was no longer on this earth.

Joey was a mistake. He had been delivered to the doorstep of Tom and Mildred Grex one spring night at no telling what time and found by Millie when she left for work before daylight. A little blanket-clad baby with no note and no clothes but with a dirty diaper. Millie nearly screamed when she found him. Tom, whose smile lit up any room he was in, well, lit up the room. Joey's new older brother bubbled with the excitement of a first grader who just scored the winning run. Who was he? No one ever found out. And in those easier times before the monstrous government of today, Tom and Millie Grex had a new son, and Johnny had the little brother that he secretly had wished for. He was taken to the hospital where Millie worked, and the police were called. But Tom already knew that he would keep him, and Millie, who was never convinced that someone wouldn't come for him someday, tried not to get too excited. Johnny would never quit bragging excitedly over his new little brother.

Joey was healthy. Doctor Wilson saw to that, but the local and state police, with the help of the FBI, never learned who he really was. So Joey had no name, no family history, and no parents until Tom and Millie hired Joe Benson, attorney-at-law. And since no one seemed to care, his parents were now Tom and Millie Grex. His family history had an interesting twist, and he had a new name, Ben Joey Grex. Tom wanted to call him BJ, but with Millie, Johnny, and the rest of his in-laws calling him Joey, he was overruled. He still called him BJ, but no one else did. He was named for his new great-grandfather, Ben Grex, a quarter Choctaw Indian, and maternal uncle, Joey Langston, the one who didn't come home from the recently ended Korean conflict.

Tom Grex said the loss of Joey Langston was a waste. Later, after studying that debacle, Joey Grex would agree. But Joey would feel that way. Like his new father, he was somewhat a hawk. He thought that if you started something you should finish it. That war was still not over! The recently deceased Joey Langston thought somewhat differently. He was an avowed anticommunist. A graduate of Tulane University, where he was cadet commandant of the ROTC program, he entered the army and was commissioned in June 1951. He came home in a coffin that November with a Silver Star. Both his father and his brother-in-law would never forgive the government for his loss. The Allies had destroyed Japan and Germany in WWII. How could they have let North Korea and China have a stalemate?

But Joey Langston is not the subject matter here. Joey Grex is and will be.

According to Dr. Wilson, Joey was about six months old that spring day, so he was arbitrarily given the birth date November 3, but no one really knew. He was obviously Irish, not only the light red hair but some freckles that faded with age gave that much away. He also had a terrible temper that he constantly kept in check. His new family, on both sides, were as easy to get along with as any people could be. Being around them taught him not to show his foul temper, and he learned that he, like his father, could light up a room with just a smile. This worked when he was in trouble or someone needed a spiritual lift.

People grew to like him, and almost anyone was glad to have him around, especially his new paternal great-grandmother, Ginger Grex. His first years in the Grex family, he spent his days with her while Tom and Millie were at work. He was never bored with errands, although he was glad when either of his parents picked him up. He was also glad to see his Granny.

Granny was somewhat mischievous. Her sense of humor could sometimes be frightening. She taught Joey to ride a bicycle by the time he was four years of age. It was a little blue one that she bought for him at a garage sale. She worked with him every day until he was proficient.

Then one day she had him hide behind her neighbor's garage until his father came for him.

When asked where he was, she nonchalantly replied, "Oh, he's riding his bike somewhere."

After his father had gone in the house, Joey rode slowly toward Granny's house.

"Somewhere!" his father replied and ran out the door to look for him.

When he saw Joey riding toward him, he knew he had been taken again. Tom Grex never understood his grandmother's sense of humor.

Granny was also the best babysitter in the world. It was all sugar cookies, love, and learning, and yes, a little humor at Granny's house. She was his favorite person.

Joey got along well in school. He was bright and mostly cheerful—not always, just mostly. He wasn't an athlete, but he could sure lift a lot of weight for his size. He worked out regularly with his football-playing older brother, Johnny. Johnny couldn't believe how much weight Joey could lift. By the time he was ten, he could bench-press his own weight, ninety pounds. For some reason, he didn't want to play team sports though. The football coach always spoke to Joey about trying out for football. Joey just replied that he was too slow and uncoordinated for football.

RUDY AND JOEY: ORDINARY CHILDREN IN AN EXTRAORDINARY TIME

On one occasion, the coach tried to insist. He found out that insisting was not a good idea when Tom Grex found out that he put no small amount of pressure on Joey. Enough had been said about that incident. No one pressured Joey after that, except Joey knew to do what his teachers said—without question!

Joey had one driving ambition. He wanted to be a fireman, a real fireman in a large city with multistory buildings. The local volunteer fire department didn't have enough action to suit him, he thought. Maybe he was wrong; in fact, I know he was. He secretly considered fire as an enemy, perhaps a deadly one, an enemy to be conquered at any cost.

Joey's father was a volunteer fireman in this small Mississippi town. He was also a perfectionist, and the limited equipment that the department owned was always in great condition. With his mechanical talent and welding expertise, he even rebuilt a two-and-a-half-ton army surplus truck into a tanker. It held hundreds of gallons of water and had the most powerful pump that Tom Grex could find. It was modified with an electric starter and could pump itself dry in short order. Grass fires didn't stand a chance against Tom Grex and the truck everyone in town called the old supertanker!

By the time Joey was eleven, he went with his father to every fire meeting and worked with the other volunteers to maintain their ever-increasing group of fire and rescue vehicles. His father taught him the procedures for driving and operating the equipment. In a small town in the mid 1960s, a teenage volunteer fireman wasn't thought of as odd. Joey was a firefighter. He went to training with his fire company and learned proper methods. He only had one problem as a volunteer fireman. He didn't have a driving license and so couldn't drive. He could sure operate the other machinery and earned a position as head pump operator on the supertanker by the time he was fourteen. It was only then, with his official position in the fire company, that Joey began thinking of himself as a firefighter. He still dreamed of a large city and skyscrapers though.

When he was in school and the fire whistle sounded, Joey was even allowed to leave school. The school was just one block north of the fire station, and he was always the first one there. Most of the time, he even had the trucks started and the overhead doors raised by the time the other volunteers arrived. Some people even commented that fire insurance rates should be lowered since they had Joey on their department. But to Joey, the meager amount of house fires and the summer brush fires just weren't exciting enough. Oh, they sometimes were, and he always felt genuine sorrow for the people whose houses were damaged or destroyed. Also, he had one bad habit as a firefighter. If someone said that they were going to lose something irreplaceable (pictures, jewelry, etc.), Joey would try to save these things for the homeowner. His father would always have a fit when Joey risked going into a fire for something. Tom Grex was not a strict disciplinarian, but as assistant fire chief and Joey's father, his opinions about "charging a fire barehanded" were emphatic!

RUDY AND JOEY: ORDINARY CHILDREN IN AN EXTRAORDINARY TIME

So Joey grew up in this small Mississippi town with a loving family, a driving ambition to be a firefighter, and his one bad habit. He also began a study of all the buildings in the town. He drew a town map and numbered each store and home. During the summer, he would go to all the buildings and get permission to draw a floor plan and note the doors and windows of each one. He was especially interested in any building with more than one story. He studied drafting in high school and put his new skills to work. By his junior year in high school, he had a book with carefully noted plans for most of the buildings and homes that his fire company served. It would serve him well one July evening.

The fire phone rang at 8:05 p.m. The address was on Sycamore Lane. Joey wasn't in school, but he was still the first to get to the fire station. He opened the overhead doors and jumped in the rescue truck. John Alexander was just minutes behind Joey. They took the rescue truck out of the station and headed for the fire. What Joey saw when he got there was startling to say the least.

Little thirteen-year-old Sarah Lincoln was sitting on the front lawn, crying, holding out her obviously burned hands. Joey knew what had happened. Sarah had tried to put out the fire, probably fearing what her parents would think of her. Joey ran to her, and she screamed, "Molly!" His face turned white. Molly was Sarah's two-year-old sister. But Joey had just drawn the plan for this house. Sarah's parents had shown him everything, even the two girl's bedrooms.

JOE POWERS

Joey grabbed his helmet and an axe. He couldn't go barehanded. Before John Alexander could stop him, he charged the front door. The heat was stifling. The house was small, and the kitchen was in flames. Molly's room was on the other side of the kitchen, and Joey put down his visor and charged through the fire to Molly's room. The door was shut, but he just applied his fire axe to the doorknob. Molly was sitting in bed, where she had been napping. She was crying loudly, and when she saw Joey in his fire suit, she screamed. I guess that a black clad man with an axe would scare anyone.

Joey kicked the door closed behind him and began knocking her window out with his axe. Despite her protests, he wrapped her in the bedding and carried her out the shattered window. He walked away from the house with Molly in one arm and his "battle axe" in the other. When he got away from the house, he carefully removed the bedding from Molly's head and put up his visor. "It's me, Molly. Joey Grex," he said. Molly went from screaming to a cute little grin. Little girls are precious.

The Lincoln home was severely damaged. But Gary and Sharon Lincoln couldn't stop talking about Joey. Gary had gotten home just as Joey was coming around the house with Molly. Two firemen were restraining him. A father would charge a fire for his children, like Joey did. One other person was in the small crowd, the news photographer. Joey's picture was on the front page. He was glad it was summer and he wasn't in school. People called him a hero. How embarrassing!

RUDY AND JOEY: ORDINARY CHILDREN IN AN EXTRAORDINARY TIME

So Joey Grex became the butt of many jokes around the fire station. He knew also that he was looked upon with respect that was earned. It was not because he was the assistant chief's son, but because he was a firefighter, the kind that most volunteer fire departments had—not a hero, just a firefighter. But Joey Grex would be a hero and not just with this fire; there would be another.

Joey finished the summer with two major grass fires. No, it was not the fires like they had in California or on the Great Plains, but still with the dry heat and no rain for over a month, this county was dry! Tom Grex helped Joey maintain the supertanker for what would be a massive rural fire at the end of July. It was an obvious arson. Arsonist were also enemies to Joey Grex.

At the end of a short dirt road just outside town, the first fire started on the south end of J. R. Stewart's hayfield. The grass was dry and burned readily. It jumped the highway and raced toward the Caufields' dairy farm. That was when Joey and his father caught up with it. When they got ahead of it and on the field, Joey saw the cattle bunched against the far fence. If they couldn't stop this fire quickly, the animals would suffer. Tom Grex drove the supertanker parallel to the fire, at a safe distance, and Joey sprayed water ahead of the fire line. Then they backed away and let the fire burn up the soaked grass. With a lack of suitable fuel, the fire died, and they drove along the fire line, putting out the rest of the fire. I will tell you that Mr. Caufield still thinks that anyone named Grex is a hero to him. He lost a little pasture temporarily but no buildings or livestock. Mrs. Caufield brought Joey a pie to the fire station. It was an embarrassment, but that didn't take anything away from the taste!

The second grass fire came from the highway. It was set by an arsonist. The old Werner spread, as everyone called that area, was ablaze. When the call came in, it was already a mile wide. This wasn't going to be as easy as the one before. The fire chief was on vacation, so Tom Grex had to manage the fire. John Alexander and Joey got the supertanker ahead of the west end and started along ahead of the fire line. They wet the brush ahead of the line for about a quarter mile. They backed up and waited for the fire to reach where they had sprayed, then they went to the fire line and put out the most troubling area near town.

A local construction company brought two bulldozers and began building a firebreak on the north side. The fire department had a small tanker, and they stayed near the construction men to keep the fire from jumping their firebreak. The east side of the fire, with little trouble, jumped a county road and suddenly was a bigger problem. John and Joey took the supertanker to the fire station to refill it. By the time they got back, it was bigger than before. When it jumped the county road, it landed in another hayfield and headed east. This wasn't going to be fun. It wasn't. The firemen fought fire until the following noon before they got it under control. It was, up until that time, the hardest fire to control in anyone's memory. It wouldn't be the last, as you will see.

RUDY AND JOEY: ORDINARY CHILDREN IN AN EXTRAORDINARY TIME

The next Saturday, Joey went to see his granny. She looked at him with dull eyes when he came in. She was sitting leaned over to the left in her chair. She couldn't talk. She only nodded her head and mumbled something he couldn't understand. He called an ambulance. Joey Grex, even with his EMT training and experience was no match for a stroke. He would never hear the fun voice or experience the interesting humor of Granny Ginger Grex again. For the rest of her life, she would not recognize Ben Joey Grex. Joey, on the other hand, would never forget her. After three weeks in the hospital, there was little anyone could think to do. Ginger Grex was put in the local nursing home. Tom and Millie tried to visit her daily, and Joey was there every day. When the family got together for holidays, they tried to bring her home. It didn't work. She didn't know anyone, nor could she enjoy any get-togethers.

The nursing home was a gentle place though. The staff always welcomed Joey and told him all they could about Granny. A semiretired preacher held services on Sunday in the recreation room. Most of the time, Joey was there, going to church with Granny as he always did. He knew she didn't understand, but sometimes she smiled when the preacher finished his sermon. Then Joey would wheel her back into her room and kiss her on the cheek. Joey finally understood what depression was.

The fire started in a small closet where supplies were kept. No one noticed soon enough because it was 4:00 a.m. The fire then broke out into the hall. It was out of control too soon. Two of the orderlies used every fire extinguisher they could get their hands on while the nurses called the fire phone and began evacuating the ambulatory patients. When Joey and the rest of the fire company got there, the fire hoses were connected, and they entered the north entrance. The nurses and aides told them that the south end needed evacuating. The fire chief and John Alexander and three other firefighters went to do that chore. Tom and Joey Grex began carrying people out of the north end, while Bill and Tom Johnson, the only two people who hated fire as much as Joey, began streaming water into the hall.

Joey kept bringing people out, the hospital staff emptied the emergency room of supplies, and all available nurses came to the scene. As soon as someone was evacuated, a member of the hospital staff or an aide from the nursing home was assigned to them. Doctor Wilson came and oversaw this medical nightmare. The two staff doctors from the nursing home were there shortly and were invaluable. They recognized the patients and rattled off information on each case.

Joey broke away from the fire and went to each patient. Then it came to him. He hadn't seen Granny. He went back in where the Smith brothers and his father were sill streaming water on the fire. "Dad, have you seen Granny? Her room is down there, but I haven't seen her!" shouted Joey. And Joey Grex charged the fire barehanded. His father tried to catch him, but Joey ran through the flames. They saw

RUDY AND JOEY: ORDINARY CHILDREN IN AN EXTRAORDINARY TIME

him enter Granny's room, but that area of the frame building collapsed. Tom Grex cried, and the whole town cried with him. They weren't found until the next day. Joey was holding his Granny Ginger under her bed, where they quietly died together.

Johnny Grex walked away from his brother's grave. He no longer bubbled with the enthusiasm of being an older brother. Johnny sobbed unashamedly.

> Walking in the sugar maple grove,
> where once the cattle grazed.
> Now many trees are raised
> in the sugar maple grove.
>
> A long, long time ago,
> only one tree rose
> at the edge of the field.
> That is now the sugar maple grove.
>
> The cattle were sold.
> No need for hay,
> Nor yet a place for the cattle to graze.
> Now the sugar maples grow.
>
> Has progress stopped?
> The farm is no more,
> maybe so.
>
> But progress is what you see
> there in the sugar maple grove.

RUDY

The first time I saw her, I was on the way to the corner store. A little black girl with a pacifier in her mouth watched me as I walked by, and I watched her. Strange it is, how little ones size each other up. She couldn't be as old as I, yet she wasn't a baby either. Still, a pacifier! And what was she doing on this side of town?

But it wasn't any of my business and I had a mission and that mission was candy! Penny candy at Charlie's Market! Where a dime would get enough treats to last a summer afternoon. I could hardly wait and hurried as fast as my short legs would carry me. On the way back, I hurried too—not to get home, but to see if the little girl was still in the yard of the home my father said was to be rented to the Worths (he a physician and she an LPN), who had been recently hired by the little hospital in our small Southern Alabama town.

And this is my first remembrance of Rudy. It will not be my last, as you will see. I would later learn that Rudy was adopted. The administrators at the hospital saw only the white professionals that were Rudy's parents. Only later would they learn that their adopted daughter was a cute little black girl. And this is how I met my first and only real friend here—my playmate for the rest of the summer and years to come.

To my father, this situation was the most humorous thing to happen here in his lifetime. He would sometimes talk about our new neighbors with admiration and respect, and other times, he would be laughing out loud at the mention of their name. My father had a strange sense of humor, one that I only now understand.

Myself

Yet I get ahead of myself. How did I get here? I hadn't always lived here. I was born at the air force base where my father was stationed in 1952 as the youngest by far of four children and the least likely to be anything important. My two sisters and my brother were honor students. From my first-grade report card, it looked like I might pass, if I was lucky.

My father was born in this Southern town as the son of a successful lawyer and his "socialite wife" (someone else's words), and from the start, my father's relationship with Grandpa was less than cordial. My father preferred the company of whomever and whenever and the building of cars and speedboats and, yes, even barns to the study of any kind of law. Although he was in the upper part of his class at school, he said it was because there was no upper class here! He left the air force in 1959 and briefly studied for an engineering degree before quitting for a job to support his ever-needy family. It looked like we would always live in southern Kansas, where my father worked as a machinist. Then early one morning, the phone rang.

When the phone rings at the wrong time, something is wrong! And this time was no different, only worse. Grandpa was gone. My father stood shocked and still. Many questions went unanswered, and with a sad goodbye, he hung up. Grammy needed him. My siblings' friends were to be left behind; we were moving home.

Home? What made me think of this little town as home was never clear. My father grew up here, and my Grandpa and Grammy Hood lived here. My mother's parents lived here too. I never lived here and had only vacationed here briefly one time before. But home it was to me—the only place I ever really wanted to be.

Dad went immediately to be with Grammy. Mother and the rest of our family stayed behind to settle things and get ready for what my siblings dreaded—a move! It was something my two older sisters would always think of with some contempt. It

RUDY AND JOEY: ORDINARY CHILDREN IN AN EXTRAORDINARY TIME

wasn't easy for two rather popular girls to leave what they thought of as home, but move we did back to this small Alabama town with the "deep South" identity and where my father was still well liked but little understood.

So there I was, at least for now, with my penny candy habit and the tools of my trade. Did I mention my trade? I was a mechanic. No, not a real one, but the only seven-year-old who got socket sets and pliers for his birthday and the only seven-year-old who could fix any bicycle, even the ten-speed variety. These were rare in this town, but they did exist, and I was the only person who had an interest in their operation.

So I was the little boy who fixed things. See, if you can work on a bicycle, you can also fix other things. And this was what I liked to do. I should also mention, this made me many friends who would otherwise ignore a little kid who didn't play ball, didn't do well in school, and wasn't very social. The older kids knew where to get a flat fixed, a chain tightened, a wheel straightened, and such things that befell your chief method of transportation when you didn't have a driver's license. Also, my fees were very gentle, Grammy said with a laugh. Well, I guess she was right. Some penny candy or bubble gum would pay for a lot of wrench twisting.

I also had another vocation. When no one needed my help and I got lonely, I played with cars—not real cars, but toy cars that I rolled along my makeshift town, that had cigar boxes for buildings and roads graded with my hands and enough dust to make even a greasy mechanic seem dirty!

After our move, I settled in to build a little life for myself. I fixed my brother's bike in the front yard so that I would be seen. I needed to let people know that I could do these things if I was to get along here. My brother was somewhat doting and would let me work on his bike even if it didn't need fixing. I guess he was proud of me, though sometimes it didn't seem that way. But nonetheless we got along well as long as I did things his way and didn't have his bike torn into a thousand pieces when he needed it.

Then most importantly, I got to know Rudy Worth, a tiny five-year-old black girl with white parents who liked to play cars, build make-believe towns, and watch a seven-year-old mechanic fix bicycles.

School, the First Day

Well, it was August and time to start second grade. It wouldn't be something I looked forward to and was even less a perfect day for my sisters. A new school shouldn't be fun, I guess. But it didn't bother me. I wasn't going to like any school, new or not! My brother found out from some of his new friends that he would be able to play sports, so he looked forward to it. Besides, he had three new friends who lived nearby, and they had spent the summer fishing and playing ball. I tried to play, but it was a laugh. "JB is not an athlete," most people would say, and they were right.

RUDY AND JOEY: ORDINARY CHILDREN IN AN EXTRAORDINARY TIME

I saw Rudy the first day. She was a cute little kindergartener with a yellow eye patch to match her yellow overalls. Things were a little tight that first day. I didn't understand why. My father would have to explain that Rudy was the first black child to enroll at the white school in this little town with the Southern identity. What difference would it make who went to school here? A lot to some people. But at the time, what did it matter to me? Rudy was perhaps my only real friend, the person who played cars with me and didn't need me to fix anything for her. I waited outside for her at recess—an undersized white kid with a cigar box full of toy cars. When the kindergarteners were released, she came directly to me, and we began to build a new "town" next to the fence. I had no idea what I had done, but apparently, I had already offended someone.

A rather large fourth grader by the name of Brent Williams came over to where Rudy and I were playing. "That your girlfriend?" he sarcastically remarked. "No, that's Rudy," I retorted. Well, second graders shouldn't sass the older kids, but I didn't know that. He frowned, looked at his companions, and they jumped on both of us! Well, I was not much of a fighter, and I was not very big, but I did have a Hood temper. I hit Brent as hard as I could, which wasn't very hard. I tried to get between Rudy and the other two and only succeeded in knocking her down. The three larger boys landed on top of us and were giving us both a good thrashing when my brother, Will, and his three friends, Edward and Edwin (twin brothers) and Jared, entered the fray. Now Will was probably not that tough, but he was a sixth grader who liked his little brother and tolerated his friends, any of them. Ed, Win, and Jared were big for their age, and although they attended the same Baptist church that my parents and grandparents attended, I soon learned they were due to watch in a fight. The three fourth-grade boys didn't last long.

I grabbed Rudy by the hand and pulled her away from the ruckus. I turned to get back in it myself when I realized that she was crying. I didn't know what to do. I will tell you that she was my friend, and I didn't like to see her cry. I picked up several rocks, and as my brother and his friends pushed my antagonists away, I threw rocks at them. I couldn't throw very well, but a rock hurts when it hits. This was all the duty teacher saw—me, a new kid, rocking three hometown boys! So this was how my first trip to see Mr. James, the principal, was arranged. It probably wouldn't be my last "trip to the office," but at the time I couldn't have cared less.

Mr. James

Mr. James was really something special. I didn't know it at the time though. He graduated from high school with my father, and Dad always spoke highly of him. He was the ruler of the dreaded "office." He questioned me as if I were a criminal. Although I tried to explain, my adrenaline was still running, and all I could do was rattle. I even told him that I would get even with Brent and his friends if it took me the rest of my life! I didn't guess he had a choice, but I really didn't appreciate the spanking. I fumed the rest of the day, and as usual, it was difficult to pay attention in class. My first day at school was a disaster. So what? My first day anywhere was never very different. I will tell you one thing though. Mr. James seemed rather happy about something. Did he enjoy giving me a spanking? I didn't think so. But what was it?

I can tell you another thing. As I fixed Rudy's eye patch over her bad eye and tried to console her, I felt something that I didn't understand. I was so mad that someone would hurt her that I couldn't get over it. She looked at me and tried to smile. She was the bravest little five-year-old I ever saw.

Lunch

When lunchtime came, Rudy was in the lunchroom, at a table by herself. The teachers tried not to notice, but I did. At the time, I could only think how lucky I was. I could sit with my friend. We sat at the table by ourselves and talked about the fight. For three days, we could think of little else. I apologized for knocking her down. She looked down and started to cry again. I was still too young to understand. I hoped that Brent's bicycle fell apart. I knew where he couldn't get any repair work done.

Ms. Estelle and Mr. A. D. after school

School was finally over for the day. I walked quietly home by myself. Ms. Worth offered me a ride, but I refused. I didn't know why. I had failed my friend and wasn't very social as usual. Rudy looked okay though. She had her pacifier back in her mouth. She took it out smiled and waved at me. The school day was ending on a positive note at least.

When I got home, I went to the garage and started to clean and rearrange my toolbox. It was what I did when I needed to think. But thinking got me nowhere. I was still mad about my first day in school. I will tell you that I am the kind who carries a grudge. And just the thought of Rudy crying and seeing her overalls grass stained and her eye patch torn off was almost more than I could take. But take it I did, but not in stride. I got permission from my youngest sister, Marlene, to ride my bicycle. I went down the lane to Ms. Estelle's.

Estelle is A. D.'s wife. A. D. is the black caretaker of the Hood farm. They were the nicest people I had ever met, and if I needed to cool off from a temper tantrum, this was where I went. Ms. Estelle made the mistake of asking how school was. I was never very good at giving a short answer. I told her about the fight and how mad I was. She smiled at me, gave me a sugar cookie, and said, "JB, as long as Rudy is your friend, this sort of thing will happen." I thought she was talking about Rudy being a girl. I would find out later what she really meant.

RUDY AND JOEY: ORDINARY CHILDREN IN AN EXTRAORDINARY TIME

While I was there, Estelle asked if I could change a light bulb for her. She always had a way of knowing what would cheer me up. I changed the bulb and dusted off the lampshade for her. She hugged me, which was always embarrassing when someone was around, but no one was around, so I hugged her back and left for home. On the way, I met Mr. A. D., who always talked to me as if I were an adult. He asked me to come around on Sunday afternoon. His grandson, Arthur, was bringing his bicycle over for repair. Mr. A. D. wanted me to bring my toolbox and help him fix it. I will tell you, it pays to have friends!

The Rest of Grade School

Rudy and I were still friends throughout our tenure in grade school. I continually got in fights with other students. Mostly, they were older, and I never came out very well. I was a regular in Mr. James's office. He would smile and say, "Well, J. B., you again?" Then he would sometimes laugh, and often enough, I wouldn't get as much punishment as I would have thought. I was afraid that my father would punish me for my indiscretions. But all he would say about my problems with school was "You'll be all right, J. B." When I got in trouble for anything else, he would be the first to punish me, but when a fight developed over Rudy, he was immediately on my side. It was something my mother would never understand.

"Why are you always fighting?" she would ask. I never could answer properly. Usually, when she asked me, I had such a good "mad on" that I could only fume and say my byword, "Groush!" It wasn't a curse word, and I was the only one who used it, but still my mother didn't like it. I was an enigma to her, though I didn't even know what the word meant at the time—not like the rest of her children, not like my "easy to get along with" father, not like my industrious sisters, and not near an athlete like my brother. Some people, both black and white, even called me strange, but not in front of my father or Mr. A. D.

Dr. and Mrs. Worth

Rudy's parents were a mystery to me. For years, they tolerated me. I sometimes expected them to forbid her from seeing me. After all, I was always in trouble at school and never a good student. Rudy, on the other hand, was bright and articulate. Despite being two years younger than me, she helped me with my schoolwork. It was sometimes embarrassing, although any excuse to hang around with her was a good excuse. Dad said something about me being easy to get along with for certain people—not everyone, just some people. I sure hoped that he meant Dr. and Ms. Worth.

RUDY AND JOEY: ORDINARY CHILDREN IN AN EXTRAORDINARY TIME

Junior High

Junior High—not my finest hour, no playground to play cars on, and no Rudy to laugh with. I will tell you that I wasn't going to like this—most likely even less than grade school. But I was surprised. No one paid much attention to me unless they needed something fixed. See, I was still the boy who fixed things. My fees had changed somewhat, but I still worked cheap. At school, I didn't ask anything for the little jobs I did. No one seemed to notice that I still liked penny candy. I didn't have as many fights and even enjoyed some of my classes, not very much though. I made it through seventh and eighth grades without too much difficulty.

I looked for full-time work after eighth grade. I thought a fourteen-year-old mechanic could find a job. Not even! None of the local businessmen would even talk to me. Oh well, I still fixed bicycles and did odd jobs. I even branched out into lawnmowers with my father's help. It provided me spending money, and I didn't have to ask my parents for much. I was getting interested in real cars. My father worked as a machinist in the engine plant in town. He taught me about electrical wiring, and I helped him when he fixed cars for people after he got home from work. I still got new tools for my birthday and Christmas, and my toolbox was now too big to carry on my bicycle.

My mother's father, Papa, had found an old craftsman toolbox for me. He had taken it apart, cleaned and painted it, and brought it to me. Now I had enough room for all my tools. I thought I looked like a professional when I did a job. I was busy that summer, and ninth grade sneaked up on me, but not before I spent most of the summer, when I wasn't fixing something, at Papa's farm.

Papa and Mama Livingston, A. D., and Estelle Darmon

I should tell you about this pair of irascible old couples. Since you already know who A. D. and Estelle are, I will start with Papa and Mama. Papa, like A. D., was a farmer. That was all he did. And with his friend A. D., they were a two-man grocery company. Papa had 160 acres of bottom land. It seemed that all he ever did amounted to taking advantage of this land. Squash, okra, beans and tomatoes, turnip greens, peppers, peas, and potatoes—these men can produce any kind of food. Papa retired in 1964; it was hard to tell though. He raised more vegetables than ever before; only now he disposed of them differently. He and Mr. A. D. had a vegetable stand near his house. He and Mr. A. D. were the best of friends, an odd situation in this time of seeming hatred between the races.

Mama Livingston was something else. She was one of those people who could cook, sew, make a lunch in a minute, and still play softball. I think she was a bit prejudiced, but she tried not to show it. At least, she and Ms. Estelle got along all right. Sometimes the two couples visited one another, causing some talk to develop on both sides of town. It didn't bother Bell Livingston or A. D. Darmon though. They laughed about how much tongue wagging they caused.

War, a Cause for Friendship

They were raised in this small town but seemed not to know each other until WWI. Things got a little dicey in the trenches of Europe. Papa was a corporal in the infantry, and A. D., a private in a supply co. But the first time they saw each other in France, they recognized each other. A. D. made sure that Papa's squad had whatever they needed, and Papa made sure that his squad treated A. D. with the respect he deserved. "Need something?" Papa would always say. "Call A. D. Darmon, and you won't be long in having it." It was the truth if I ever heard it.

Their friendship was tested once. Never again. Some people were saying that A. D. was somewhat "uppity," whatever that meant. A group decided to pay him a visit. Word gets around in a small town though. When they got to Mr. A. D.'s place, what they found was a kindly farmer asking if they wanted to stay for supper. They started to tell him off but stopped when he pulled his shotgun from behind the door.

"You think that will stop all of us?" one man shouted. "No," said Papa from the side of the outbuilding, "but this Springfield rifle will take care of anyone left over." Now facing two old armed veterans is not something you want to do. I don't care who you are or how many there are of you!

After that little incident, everyone left them alone. It was a good thing too. These were the wrong kind of people to stir up—too nice to bother anyone, too ornery to allow anyone to bother them.

And to this day, they still did what they always wanted to do—farm. Mr. A. D. raised fruit and hogs, Papa raised vegetables and a few cattle, and they both took care of the corn patch. When Mr. A. D. weaned his pigs, he brought them to Papa. Papa fed them out, and they got together after the first frost and killed hogs. Papa sugar-cured the hams and made bacon. A. D. ground the meat and made the best sausage in the world. They could sell all this but didn't. "This is for family and friends," they would say. Funny it was how two men from different sides of town sounded like each other. They were more like relatives than friends.

I think this is where I got the idea of charging penny candy for work. These two had a different sweet habit. The two old geezers knew how to get a different kind of treat. Now when Ms. Parsons, a white widow with two children, came to the farm to buy vegetables, they always picked out the best they had. They loaded a sack with whatever she asked for and then some. When she asked how much, it didn't make any difference what she had, her bill was always one dollar, even for five dollars' worth of vegetables. And they had another trick up their sleeve. Mr. A. D.'s fruits were not always in season, but they seemed

RUDY AND JOEY: ORDINARY CHILDREN IN AN EXTRAORDINARY TIME

to always have a bag of apples that they offered to her children. "Looks like this pair could use a pie," one of them would say as he handed the apples over to the little girls. I once wondered what was going on. Were these old men flirting with Ms. Parsons?

Well, yes, but not in the way you would think.

There was another widow, a tall black lady introduced to me as Ms. Emma, with five children. Ms. Emma patronized their vegetable stand regularly. She would pick out even more vegetables, and her bill was also one dollar. And to top this off, they would have a sack of peaches for her children. The first time I saw this, I didn't understand. But I would.

If you were at their vegetable market the next day, everything would be made plain. Ms. Parsons would drive by and drop off an apple pie for them—a wonderful creation with brown sugar, cinnamon, and pieces of red hot candy. And Ms. Emma would always walk over from her house, which was close by, with a peach cobbler—the best one you ever saw or tasted, with sugar on the crust and caramel candy melted in the peach filling. Now as I said before, word got around, and when these two ladies were seen headed toward the vegetable stand, the barbershops on both sides of town would empty out; sometimes even the barbers would lock up and come. At first, they tried to feign some reason for being there. But eventually, that even ceased. They came for one reason—pie!

And about a dozen old men, white and black, would sit around, eating pie and talking about the weather, gardening, or fishing. This was always, I thought, the best party in town. I asked Papa if he wasn't taking advantage of these two nice ladies. "Well, in a way, I guess we are," he replied. "But if we gave them the vegetables, they would think they were taking advantage of us. This way, they get anything we have to offer in the way of help, but it doesn't seem to them they are getting a handout, understand?" I guess I did, and boy, did I enjoy the pie! But eventually, the best of times ended, and school did start.

Ninth Grade

The first day of school of ninth grade was to be a grand day. Rudy was in seventh grade! I had my friend close again. I tried to talk to her whenever I had the chance. She wasn't a little girl anymore though. It seemed like overnight she had become something different. She came to school with a blue eye patch and a blue blouse to match. She was beautiful! She had made a few friends among the her white classmates. She didn't seem as interested in the skinny white kid. Oh well, I now knew what it must have been like for her when I left grade school. We had been inseparable. Sometimes, I felt lost without her, but what could I do?

Groush!

Integration

Tough times were coming for our little town. I didn't see the problem, but it came without warn-

RUDY AND JOEY: ORDINARY CHILDREN IN AN EXTRAORDINARY TIME

ing. The black and white school districts were integrated. Being unsociable had its disadvantages. No one talked to me about anything. Most of the other students knew about my friendship with Rudy. It was expected that I wouldn't join the fight against total integration of our school.

They were wrong though. I didn't want integration either, but not for the reason you think though.

If the black students came to our school, I would probably lose any chance to continue my friendship with Rudy. At least these were my thoughts on the subject. She would probably like kids who were her color, not dumb old J. B. Hood. But integration came, and with it the resulting problems.

The problems for me were somewhat different. I was still a social weakling. My friends were few and none close. My brother and his friends had graduated. Except for Rudy, I was basically friendless. But my turn in racial trouble was coming. On the first day that black students enrolled, I had a chance to talk to Rudy in the hall.

A blustering black student about twice my size came by and asked me, "That your girlfriend?"

"No, that's Rudy," I said harshly.

"Sister, what are you doing hanging around this boy?" he said to Rudy.

"That's J. B.," Rudy remarked, "and he *is* my friend!"

Well, as you can imagine, the fight started. I got the worst of it as usual. I also got to see the principal.

J. B. Hood, the troublemaker, was back to his old self.

It was expected that white kids were going to be all the problem. I was white, so I was thought to be the antagonist. Besides, my reputation always preceded me to the office. I took the punishment but not in stride. I still was the best person in town at carrying a grudge. Later, I haltingly tried to apologize to Rudy. "Well, J. B., for a guy who fixes things, you sure know how to fix a fight. You just hit someone in the fist with your face!" she replied. Then she smiled and said, "You're my best friend, J. B., and I love you." I didn't think anything had ever sounded so good.

There was an upside to this incident. Rudy started paying more attention to me. She smiled sweetly every time she saw me and spent more time talking to me between classes. I liked Rudy even more. She was growing up, but she still seemed the little girl who was my friend. There was only one problem. When someone asked if she was my girlfriend, I wanted to say yes but didn't. I didn't have any idea how to have a girlfriend. I still had zero social skills. If I wasn't around Rudy, Mr. A. D. and Ms. Estelle, my family, or someone who needed something fixed, I was an outcast. About all I could say was "No, that's Rudy!" She was the only girl who ever paid any attention to me. When I was younger, it didn't bother me, but now, I guess I was feeling isolated.

RUDY AND JOEY: ORDINARY CHILDREN IN AN EXTRAORDINARY TIME

The Dance

At the end of ninth grade, a dance was always scheduled. I didn't think much about this although it was the talk of the freshmen class. I couldn't dance and never attended any parties. What would a person like me do at a dance? All the boys and girls tried carefully to find a date.

There was talk of trouble because this was the first dance that would include blacks and whites. I was sure that I would just stay home and avoid the embarrassment. That was all over with when I walked home from school on Tuesday. Rudy asked if I would walk her home. That was easy. I always wanted to be with her! The small talk was easy as she was my best friend. I was unprepared for what happened when we got to her house though. She asked me to stay awhile.

Ms. Worth fixed us a Coke and said, "Where have you been, J. B.? I haven't seen you for some time." I stumbled over my reply as usual. It was always difficult to talk to people, and Ms. Worth rarely needed any repair work. I was just unable to have a conversation with anyone, it seemed.

Rudy wanted to sit on the porch and talk. "J. B.," she spoke softly, "are you going to the dance?"

"I can't dance," I replied.

"I wish I could go," she said.

I looked at her and blurted out, "If you want to go, I'll take you!" Never had I seen such a smile.

"Do you mean it?" she said in an excited voice.

I was trapped. I always do what I say I will do, and now I had spoken the improbable! J. B. Hood, the boy who couldn't dance and couldn't get along with anyone, had asked a girl for a date! I felt lucky that it was Rudy. Anyone else would have laughed at me.

Well, word gets around. Not only was J. B. Hood going to a dance, but he had a date with a black girl! See, not many seventh graders get to go to the freshman dance. And even though Rudy was going with stupid old J. B., she was going. Although I didn't know it at the time, there was some jealousy developing—with Rudy's classmates, because she was going; the black kids, because she was going with me; and the rest of town, because a mixed-race couple would be there.

Whatever I did, it seemed to cause a problem.

Groush!

The rest of the week, I spent working, hoping to have enough money for my date with Rudy. I told my father about what I had gotten myself into.

He laughed and said, "Don't worry, J. B. What funds you don't raise, I'll make up for you."

So I quit worrying and resolved to do the best I could. I finished a bicycle I was rebuilding, a Sting-Ray model, and sold it to Mr. A. D. for his youngest grandson. I hated to charge him for it, but he seemed happy to get it and counted out the money with a smile.

"You're a good mechanic, J. B. I'd rather have this bike than a new one," he said. It does pay to have friends, don't you think?

RUDY AND JOEY: ORDINARY CHILDREN IN AN EXTRAORDINARY TIME

I went to all my neighbors and asked for repair work, the first time in my life that I had solicited work. Normally, I would just wait until I was asked to fix something. My parents took me shopping, and by Saturday night, I was ready, as ready as I would ever be.

When my oldest sister, Nicolette, who was in for the weekend, took me to pick up Rudy, I was shocked, to say the least. My best friend looked like a model. Now Rudy's favorite color was yellow, that much I knew, and since that was all I knew, I had asked Ms. Estelle to make her a corsage from a yellow flower. Luck, sometimes, even came to dumb old J. B. Rudy wore a black full-length dress with a yellow wrap and a yellow sash. As usual, her eye patch matched, making her look older than her thirteen years. I was too nervous to pin on her flower, so Ms. Worth pinned it on.

She was stunning to say the least!

With a promise that Nicolette would have us home shortly after the dance was over, we left. What did a guy like me do at a dance? For one thing, be with the prettiest girl there, at least in my opinion. I didn't value my opinion except when it came to my best friend.

Our entrance to the banquet did not go unnoticed. I wasn't paying any attention to anyone or anything save Rudy. But we were getting some attention from both sides of the gym. The black students were glaring at us, and the white students were looking at me with what amounted to disdain. I still was too naive to realize this. Remember, I had no social skills, and now that I think about it, I don't want any!

There was one thing that I learned rather quickly—the girls, both black and white, were intent on having a good time. They bantered back and forth and danced with one another. The black boys would dance, but the whites were reluctant, so the girls just danced with one another.

I stood with Rudy, holding her hand, not sure what to do. Finally, she just joined the group of girls who were dancing. She could dance, and so could her friends. I couldn't, and I knew it. But even dumb J. B. had some luck. When a slow number came on, Rudy dragged me on to the floor and made me try. Holding her close was about the best feeling in the world. Oh bother, as luck would have it, we were getting too much attention again. I didn't see what was happening at first, only the approach of the Darmon brothers.

No, they were not brothers. One was white, the other black. Both were football players and bigger than most ninth graders. Arthur Darmon was Mr. A. D.'s grandson, and Julian Darmon was the son of the bank vice president. There was a story that Julian's ancestors owned Arthur's ancestors, and that was how they came to have the same last name. When they first met, an uneasy peace developed.

Football started, and a mutual respect was founded. Then as the school year progressed, they became inseparable and were kiddingly called the Darmon brothers. The Darmon brothers nickname was always used with respect around either one of them though. Their approach didn't bother me. I had been their bicycle mechanic since grade school. They were as close as I had to friends although they rarely had time for me except when they needed something fixed.

The trouble was coming from a different direction. Two students wanted Rudy to dance with them. No, they didn't want to dance with Rudy; they were looking for trouble. Dumb old J. B., a white kid with a black girl on his arm, watched their approach and stood quietly while they demanded her attention.

"I'm with J. B.," she said.

This didn't go well. The next thing I knew, one of them grabbed Rudy, and I became J. B. Hood.

I spoke sharply, "Leave her alone!"

"What you going to do about it?" was the reply.

"He ain't gonna do nothing" came a stern voice from behind me. "We are!" The Darmon brothers! They were a combined weight of about four hundred pounds taking up for J. B. Hood. I can tell you again that it pays to have friends, even ones you don't know were your friends.

One of the sponsors came over to see what was going on. "Nothing at all," responded Arthur. "We're just visiting with these two," said Julian. And that was that. With the Darmon brothers watching out for us, Rudy and I had no more trouble. Dances that you didn't know you wanted to go to just didn't last long enough!

At the door, old "no social skills" still didn't know what to do. Rudy stood on her tiptoes and kissed me on the cheek. "You may be strange," she said, "but you're my kind of strange." Then she went in her house, and I was left to return to Nicolette's car with a silly grin that I hoped no one would see. Nicolette just smiled at me and asked, "Did you have a good time?"

High School, the Fun Part

High school—well, the first two years—was like the rest of my life. Little or nothing to talk about. Rudy and I still were friends, and sometimes, when someone would see us together, remarks were made. We ignored them if possible despite my temper, and mostly the people with the stupid vocabularies were stopped when someone would tell them ominously, "That's John Hood's boy" or "That's A. D. Darmon's friend." If Mr. A. D. or Papa's name came up, quiet usually ensued.

Everyone knew the story about the night at Mr. A. D.'s house, and no one wanted trouble with them, even if they were just two old farmers.

I finally landed a part-time job at the engine plant where my father worked. It bothered me some that he had to get me a job, but it was a job, and it allowed me to take Rudy to lunch sometimes or to the occasional movie. We had to be careful though. Sometimes the Darmon brothers weren't around.

RUDY AND JOEY: ORDINARY CHILDREN IN AN EXTRAORDINARY TIME

I still got into fights, and I still generally came out on the short end, but who cared? Most people knew that I would fight now, so they left Rudy and me alone. This suited me fine as I got tired of Rudy saying, "Oh, J. B., not again!" The fights at school also caused me to spend too much time in the principal's office. There Mr. Johnston took up where Mr. James left off. "Well, J. B. Hood, you again?" Sometimes I wondered if Mr. James had talked about me to him. I seemed never to get the punishment I expected, and most of the time, when I appeared, he would start laughing. I didn't think being in the office was that humorous.

I still heard the remark, "That your girlfriend?" And I still replied with the same sharp retort, "No, that's Rudy!" Now that school was integrated, Rudy also caught some flack from black students. "What are you hanging around with that white boy for?" Yet it was hard to get the upper hand with Rudy. She just replied gently or sharply as the need arose, "He's my friend!"

When I became a junior, new things began to happen. The most important thing for me was the occasional dances after football games. I wasn't afraid to ask Rudy to go with me, and her parents still allowed it. Patient and understanding—that was Rudy's parents. It was still hard to believe that such a pretty girl would go anywhere with me and even harder to believe that her parents would allow her to go. Maybe they didn't know me as well as the rest of the town. When I would go to their house, they treated me like a welcomed guest, not the troublemaker I seemed to be for most people.

I turned seventeen in the eleventh grade. Hard to believe that my sisters and brother were adults now, not the teenagers I remembered so well. Nicolette was a schoolteacher and just finished her master's degree. She was planning to be a school administrator someday. Marlene never liked college, and although she went four years, she never got a degree. She was an insurance agent in Selma, Alabama. Both of them were married, and I liked both brothers-in-law. Sometimes I thought they tolerated me because I was their wives' baby brother.

Will finished college, where he played baseball on scholarship. He coached and taught math. He wasn't married, but he had a wonderful girlfriend. Sweet and beautiful she was, and if Rudy wasn't my best friend, I think I would be jealous. I wished I was at least something like any of my siblings.

I still struggled in school, except for math. Being able to read a tape measure and calipers and add and subtract, multiply and divide whole numbers and fractions were all things you need to know to be a mechanic. And a mechanic I was. I even learned, with my father's help, to rebuild engines and, in general, repair any car. I even figured out foreign cars with their metric parts and had metric tools. Not many Subarus or Datsuns around here though. This was a part of the country that liked Detroit iron. But the ones that were here were only repaired by J. B. Hood.

RUDY AND JOEY: ORDINARY CHILDREN IN AN EXTRAORDINARY TIME

I finally got my own car. I got it by purchasing a 1960 Chevrolet with what little money I could save. I was still not very good with money or fees for my work. Ms. Parsons or Ms. Emma could get anything they wanted done for one dollar plus benefits. I liked pie too.

The Chevrolet was a gray Bel Air with a seriously injured automatic transmission. It took two months but I can now overhaul a transmission. What money I had left, after I bought the car and fixed the transmission, went to insurance. Even though my sister is an agent, insurance is high for seventeen year old drivers.

My brother came to visit after I got my car. He brought his friend Ronnie. "What have you bought J.B., A mafia hit car?" Ronnie remarked. Well, I guess it was nondescript but it had air conditioning and a radio. Most people in town didn't have air conditioned cars but I did. I didn't use the radio unless Rudy was with me. Music is just noise that some people like to hear. I like no noise. The kind of quiet you get from a well-oiled mechanism.

High School, the Not-So-Fun Part

Something happened to me that I still am not sure I believe. When I started senior year, the school changed, and so did I. Maybe I was going to grow up after all. I didn't take offense so readily when anyone made rude remarks to me. I just chuckled and ignored the idiots. Mostly they didn't press the issue, but as you might realize, some did.

People began to move into town from other areas to work in the expanded engine plant. My father said that cheap labor that was supposedly available in this area caused the parent corporation to close a plant in Flint, Michigan, and combine it with the plant that my father worked for. Our civic leaders hailed this as a grand addition to our economy. The only thing I could see that this expansion did was cause new people to move into town. Very few local people were hired to staff the expansion; they just brought more workers into the community from Flint and other areas. The town and the school grew with the new faces.

Our school also got a new superintendent, a no-nonsense man with a no tolerance policy toward behavior. I could see that the new people and the new administrator might develop into a problem for a boy with a temper like J. B. Hood. It did.

One of the new kids walked by Rudy and me. I didn't know if he was unaware of Rudy's bad eye and thought that her patch was a joke or if he was just mean. He reached for her, and before I could stop him, he yanked the patch from her head. Jeff Williams was walking by, going to baseball practice, and had his new Louisville Slugger. I just yanked it out of his hand and went to work. A skinny nobody was just a skinny nobody, but a skinny nobody with a baseball bat was due to watch. Most of the fights that I had I lost, or maybe I just held my own,

RUDY AND JOEY: ORDINARY CHILDREN IN AN EXTRAORDINARY TIME

barely. But this was different. No one bothered Rudy Worth when I was around! Anyway, I was tired of being whipped! I won handily and sent a bully out of school in an ambulance.

I broke his right hand, the one that held Rudy's eye patch, when he tried to ward off the first blow and put two knots on his head that were bigger than hen eggs just because I could. I still would have been beating him if he hadn't fallen down the stairs and both Darmon brothers and Jeff repossessed the ball bat.

The superintendent was close by, but he didn't try to stop me until Julian Darmon had the bat and Arthur Darmon was holding me. I think maybe he had heard a little about the troublemaker J. B. Hood.

"Groush!" I screamed. I wanted him to get up and fight! But the new kid wasn't getting up. I struggled to get away from Arthur, but he just held on. The superintendent told the English teacher, who appeared suddenly, to call an ambulance quickly. Arthur just held me around the waist while I screamed obscenities at this kid I barely knew. Maybe I was not going to grow up either. But if growing up meant letting Rudy be treated like that, I didn't want to grow up!

After Julian and Arthur tried to calm me down, he told me to go to the office. There was no "You again, J. B." from this character. He just expelled me from school for the rest of the year! He didn't whip me or ask me what happened. He didn't even talk to me. He told me to leave the school grounds immediately and not come back! I still had about a quart of adrenaline running through me, and I just glared at him. If I still had that ball bat, I think I would have used it again. I went to my locker, with him watching me, and retrieved my belongings, got into my car, and left. If something like this wouldn't cause your adrenaline to flow freely, I suspect that you are dead!

I didn't go home though. I drove to the engine plant where my father worked. When I got there, I thought maybe I shouldn't be here. So I went to the parking lot, found his car, and waited three hours for him to get off.

Dad came before I wanted him to, and I still didn't know how to tell him what happened. He told me to follow him home. I started to just keep on going when I drove up to our house, but I pulled in. When we went inside, he asked me to settle down and tell him what happened. I did the best I could, which wasn't very good.

Dr. Worth called, and my father talked to him for nearly thirty minutes. Then he just looked at me and smiled. "You'll be all right, J. B." was all he said. Mother was working the evening shift.

What really surprised me was that she didn't say much when she got home either.

This kind of story gets around, and I expected a real problem from her. I only learned later that Dr. and Ms. Worth had gone by to see her after they talked to Rudy. It wasn't until the next morning that I realized how upset Dad was. I would learn that no one bothered Rudy Worth when John Hood was around either. And no one bothered J. B. Hood because his father was always around.

Dad left me at home the next morning and, after calling the plant manager, drove to the school to visit the new superintendent. He had to demand to talk with the Darmon brothers and Jeff Williams. All three confirmed what I had finally been able to tell my father. Arthur even told Dad that I saved him from getting thrown out of school. "I was headed for the twerp when J. B. whacked him with that ball bat." I heard later that he just glared at the superintendent and told him, "You need to be careful around here. You're not in your hometown."

Maybe my father wasn't as easy to get along with as I thought. Certainly, the new superintendent didn't think so. He came back from his visit and talked quietly to me.

"What do you want to do now?" he asked me.

I couldn't do anything but stare at the floor. Then I said the stupidest thing, even for J. B. Hood, "I guess I'll just join the army."

"Might be a good idea," replied Dad.

The army!

So that was how I ended up in the US Army. My father thought that I needed to get away from town before anyone tried to press charges for my little scuffle. Well, it really wasn't all that small a scuffle if you think about it. I would learn later that Rudy's antagonist that I used the ball bat on had to spend the night in the hospital. He had a concussion and a broken hand. I knew his hand was broken, and I thought I had fractured his skull! Served him right.

There was only one downside to this. I didn't get to spend my senior year doing what seniors did—going to dances, football games, and movies—and with me would have been Rudy. I left town immediately after an almost tearful goodbye to Rudy, where she kissed me—with her parents watching! It was embarrassing, to say the least. Maybe she was my girlfriend. I felt as lonely as I had ever been. I would sometimes take my wallet out and stare at her picture. I still had one of her at the ninth-grade dance nearly four years ago. She was still so beautiful. I would never forget this, as it was the first time I had successfully attended a social function with kids my own age.

Sometimes I would laugh when I thought of this, as my social functions before Rudy always involved the "older kids"—my Papa and Mr. A. D. and their friends.

Yet, in the army I was, and I hoped to enjoy it as much as I could. I thought that I would end up doing some sort of mechanic work. I could just imagine working on tanks, trucks, or even helicopters. I thought that I might get to learn about diesel engines, which were a mystery to me. And getting to work on aircraft engines—this was going to be a new vocation. I thought it was the only thing I could do well, and I intended to enjoy it. Didn't happen though. The army didn't see it my way. My test scores were awful, and I ended up in the infantry! Dumb

RUDY AND JOEY: ORDINARY CHILDREN IN AN EXTRAORDINARY TIME

old J. B. Hood thinking things were going to go his way. Vietnam was all the rage, and the army needed soldiers, not bicycle mechanics.

After basic training, I went to the infantry school at Fort Polk, Louisiana. One thing that I learned fairly fast was that I was not the only person in the world without any social skills. A boy from eastern Oklahoma was in my training company. He was not like most young boys who were about to become men. Tommy Charles Walton, a twenty-one-year-old kid, was a person destined never to grow up. He would do anything he was told to do with enthusiasm, even cleaning the latrine or KP. He was a little overweight, and like me, he wasn't an athlete. He struggled mightily with the physical training. He wanted to be a soldier and to be accepted by his peers. To this end, he tried hard to meet the expectations of the drill instructors and the future soldiers in our training company. Tommy was also willing to help anyone who needed it and would carry anything for anybody on the forced marches.

He asked everyone to call him T. C., but all the other trainees called him Tommy Charles. The inclusion of his middle name was not appealing to him, but he took it well. In general, I thought that he was the real man and the people who downgraded his efforts were twerps like the ones at home. So Tommy Walton became the nearest thing I had to a friend. I was still J. B. Hood, and when someone picked on us, I took it personal. I pitched my tent with him in the field because no one else wanted to share a shelter with Tommy Charles. This relationship might prove to be a problem for me, but I dealt with problems as they came and didn't plan for them.

After training, we both were assigned to a light infantry unit stationed in Fort Riley, Kansas. I almost made it back to where my family lived before Grandpa died. When I got there, my squad leader was someone I knew—Brent Williams! I said to myself, "This isn't good."

I was wrong though. Brent just sidled up to me when I arrived at my unit area and said, "J. B. Hood, still like to fight? If you do, at least you'll get paid for it here." He surprised me, and when I turned around, he was smiling and shook my hand. "Jeff wrote me that you were in the army, but I never expected to see you. Thought you'd be chief mechanic somewhere."

So here was where I expected to finish my service time and go home. My expectations were rarely met. The army didn't normally send seventeen-year-olds to combat zones. I guess no one told the army that my unit had a seventeen-year-old soldier assigned to it. The whole unit got orders for Vietnam. Brent tried to get me to complain to the first sergeant because of my age. I was still stubborn though and just packed to ship out.

The only thing that bothered me was Tommy's enthusiasm. "This is what I've been waiting for!" he remarked almost gleefully. I was sure he didn't know enough to know what was waiting for him. I know I didn't. Brent had spent six months in the war zone. That was why he was a nineteen-year-old sergeant.

RUDY AND JOEY: ORDINARY CHILDREN IN AN EXTRAORDINARY TIME

He was wounded slightly and got a staph infection in the hospital. That short-circuited his first combat tour. He could have complained too but didn't. I was beginning to admire the boy I had fought with in grade school, and I hoped his combat experience would help us. Even I underestimated his value to Tommy and me.

Vietnam, Two Weeks That Seemed Like a Lifetime

My company commander in Vietnam was Captain Steven Thomas, a military school graduate who had a reputation for taking care of his troops. He noticed that I was still a buck private. "Hood, we have to get you promoted to something," he remarked. I didn't care if I got any rank. I just wanted to finish my time and go home. A year, one year without Rudy—let's get this over with!

When we got in the country, we were assigned to a fire base in the central highlands. The soldiers already there called it Fort Apache. I never learned if it had a real name. I'm sure it did, but I wasn't there long enough to find out. There was another fire base called Fort Apache, but that didn't seem to bother this bunch. They just said they were Indian fighters, even the Indians who were troops in all the units on Fort Apache. I thought that was a bit comical, but they didn't. I was not the only strange character in the army.

We took over the perimeter from a unit that was leaving. We didn't have to build any hooches or trenches; they were already there. Convenient was what Sergeant Brent Williams called our situation.

Things got around in Vietnam, just like at home. A new unit was in the country—an untried unit—and the Vietcong were going to try us. We got hit on the second evening.

It was still daylight when the first probe hit second platoon on the easternmost part of the perimeter. Tommy and I were on the north side, and immediately, the veterans and real soldiers on the eastern flank opened up with everything they had. They shot enough ammunition to decimate the entire army of some countries. Tommy wanted to go to the fighting. Brent sharply ordered him to stand fast. "They'll try us soon enough," he said. He was right. The little soldiers in black pajamas charged out of the tree line, which was too close for comfort. Tommy saw them before I did and opened up on full auto, and the rest of our squad picked it up. We weren't hitting them that well, but they retreated into the trees. Tommy had to be told to cease fire. A quiet ensued.

Strange after such a rattle of machine guns and automatic rifles. The quiet didn't last long enough.

The second probe on our front came with enthusiasm. They charged right out of the trees at a run. Wild Billy Wilson, a good hand with a machine gun, decimated their first wave with help from John Dalton, the best shot in our unit with any weapon. Then the mortars hit us. Why they didn't use them first was never very clear. Billy went out of action, permanently. Two of the interior reserve machine gun crews saw what was about to happen and shored up our crumbling defenses. Our mortar crews had been giving the tree line a fit and continued to send rounds toward this almost-crazed enemy. Sergeant Brent Williams set off the claymore mines he had carefully placed in front of our position. Men on both sides were dying, and Tommy Walton was getting mad—fighting mad!

He charged out of our trench, with me yelling at him to get down. He fired his weapon without aiming and made it about seventy-five yards down the hill before he first got hit.

I screamed, "Groush!" Then as he pleaded for a medic, I got mad! I scrambled down the hill toward him. I made it about thirty feet, then a bullet struck my helmet. It went flying off my head, but I just kept running. The next bullet hit me in the stomach, but I barely noticed the pain. I had almost made it to Tommy when a bullet tore through my lower leg. I noticed this immediately when the ground came up and slapped me in the face!

Now there were two of us down. Out of the perimeter and too close to the charging VC, I emptied my rifle then grabbed Tommy's and emptied it. I reloaded and emptied both rifles on full auto again. Just like at home, I was not a very effective fighter. Sergeant Brent Williams appeared, and man, was I glad to see him! He fired three round bursts carefully and accurately and held off the VC charge near us. Things didn't look very good for any of us. I tried to help but kept firing full auto and emptying both my rifle and Tommy's.

Captain Thomas saw what was happening and charged out of the command bunker with a BAR. Where did he get that thing? He and Brent moved in front of Tommy and me. With help from Captain Thomas, Brent was holding off the little black clad VC.

"Can you get up?" Brent yelled at me. I didn't know, but I grabbed Tommy and tried to carry him back up the hill. I kept falling though. I hate to mention this, but I was bleeding like a stuck hog, like the ones Papa and Mr. A. D. killed each fall.

Brent and Captain Thomas stayed forward and kept everyone off us until I made it back to the trench, dragging Tommy. Then I turned and, with help from John Dalton and his new machine gun crew, tried to cover them. I yelled at them to come on, and just as Brent made it back to the trench, a bullet took him behind the right knee. The last time I saw Captain Thomas, he was still working the enemy over with that BAR. I dragged Brent into the trench and passed out just as the air cover came in.

Cobra gunships sprayed gunfire and rockets into the trees, and air force jets dropped napalm on the north and east ends of our perimeter. But I was out of it. It was a sorry end to my first taste of combat. Captain Thomas took advantage of the air cover and crawled back with a crease in his helmet and a sprained ankle.

My unit was a mess, but according to our battalion commander, you would have thought we had

RUDY AND JOEY: ORDINARY CHILDREN IN AN EXTRAORDINARY TIME

just won the war by ourselves. We had seven dead, including Wild Bill, and twenty-three wounded, including Tommy, Brent, and me. For some reason, Captain Thomas wasn't considered to be injured. I guess you can't blame a sprained ankle on the enemy. I knew who to blame it on though: Tommy and me. The enemy didn't fair nearly as well. After dark, they tried to recover their dead and wounded. Some of our unit had night vision though. More killing, more mortar attacks, too much pain.

I ended up in the battalion aid station. I nearly jumped off the stretcher when I woke up. The medic, a sergeant with premature gray around his temples, pushed me back down and said, "Take it easy, soldier."

I had an IV stuck in my right arm and a bloody bandage on my stomach. A four-inch gash was in my hairline, and my leg was hurting so bad I wanted to cry. Tommy was next to me and didn't look any better. I couldn't see Brent and was worried. Had I pulled him into the trench? I thought so, but where was he? I almost screamed his name but managed to keep my mouth shut for a change. Medevac choppers braved enemy fire to come for the wounded. I got a trip to Saigon. It could have been under better circumstances.

Later, after Brent and I got out of surgery, he came by in a wheelchair. His knee had been destroyed when he saved Tommy and me. I felt like a dunce, a stupid idiot who caused a good man to be nearly crippled. Brent just smiled and said, "We saved your friend."

I didn't see Tommy again. He was taken stateside for more surgery on his arm and for bullet wounds to his shoulder and chest. Brent kept a good attitude and checked on me every day. It was hard to see him in the wheelchair. Sometimes he tried to cheer me up. I tried to apologize to him for Tommy and me. He laughed, not convincingly though. This good soldier went home on crutches due to a couple of idiots. I didn't think I would ever be able to forgive Tommy or me for what had happened to him.

This was the end of my combat experience—one battle. I got the Purple Heart and, believe it or not, a Bronze Star. I didn't deserve it, but with help from Captain Thomas and John Dalton's and Brent Williams's accounts of the action, I got it. Brent was awarded the Silver Star. Now if anyone valued what Sergeant Williams did for two green soldiers in his squad, that was little enough.

John came by to see me later and told me that Brent stayed in the trench and helped fend off the attack despite his knee. I never met a braver man—only nineteen years old and a real soldier.

Some men still say that in a war, uncommon valor is a common virtue. If people could have seen Sergeant Brent Williams and Captain Steven Thomas that day, they would really believe this statement.

John Dalton didn't get any medals. If you think about it, he and the two reserve machine gun crews were the ones that saved the day. They held off the enemy while Tommy and I were down and in the open.

RUDY AND JOEY: ORDINARY CHILDREN IN AN EXTRAORDINARY TIME

Captain Thomas got a letter of commendation. The army was trying to be cheap on the medals they gave the real heroes. He came by to show me his helmet. "You darn near got my head shot off!" he said with a grin. I silently wondered if he would someday be a general and treat all his soldiers like he treated me.

As it was, Brent was given his discharge and left the army. Later I would find out that it was always what he wanted to do—be a soldier. Tommy and I had destroyed his career before he turned twenty. He went home and, with his bum leg, began thinking about a new career. Groush!

Recuperation

I was given my discharge too after four months at Fort Riley, recuperating. My parents, Papa and Mama Livingston, and even Mr. A. D. and Ms. Estelle visited me one time. I wanted to cry when I saw them. I didn't feel very brave, but they praised me for saving Tommy. I tried to tell them that Brent saved us.

Brent was already home, building up my reputation though. He told everyone in town that me and the Vietcong got all the fighting we wanted, and finally, I was good at something besides being a mechanic. He downplayed his part in our rescue, but the Silver Star was not something to downplay. I promised myself I'd straighten out the story when I got home.

I had a cast on my leg for nearly eight weeks. The bullet had put a groove in the bones of my leg and fractured them. I had an infection in the wound in my stomach. I had never been in the hospital but made the best of it.

The medics in Vietnam and at Fort Riley were good to me. The got me healthy despite my ignorance. I couldn't say enough good about them to anyone who would listen. There was a difference between being treated by civilians and being treated by people who considered you a brother.

I received letters from Rudy all the time while I was in the army. I was not much to write but did manage to write back occasionally. She asked if I wanted her to come see me. I did, but I didn't tell her that. I just indicated I'd be home soon enough. It wasn't soon enough. Groush, I missed her!

Back Home

I finally got home eleven months after I joined the army—a medical discharge. I didn't think I was hurt that bad, but I didn't argue. I was homesick, mainly for Rudy.

Brent was the first person I went to see. Rudy was in school. I went to his house in the "mafia hit car." He saw me drive up and limped out to join me in the yard. I still had a hard time seeing his limping form, but he seemed in a good mood.

"Let's go for a drive," he said. And so we drove and drove and drove. We talked about what happened, and he laughed at me for trying to apologize again. Finally, he just told me a story about two men—one white, the other black—who were in WWI and came home friends. "Now you know how your Papa and Mr. A. D. feel about each other. You should know how you and I probably feel about each other," he said. I now had my first true friend, and I was proud to have him.

We went to Rudy's house after school was out. I got a nice welcome there too. She made too much over me and thanked Brent for taking care of me.

I asked if Rudy could go with Brent and me, and as usual, her parents just smiled and said, "Of course, J. B." We went to pick up Brent's friend, Rhonda Mills, and we drove and drove and drove. We went to Charlie's Market. He literally ran to greet us.

"I'm glad you're back, J. B. Penny candy sales almost went away after you left." Then he got a sack from under his counter and filled it with some of every kind of candy he had. We drank a Pepsi there and talked to him for nearly an hour. When I tried to pay him, he just laughed.

Everywhere we went, people yelled and waved at us. We stopped and talked to everyone we knew. Where did these social skills come from? Well, I was eighteen now. Was I growing up? I doubted it.

Work and Social Functions with an Eighteen-Year-Old Misfit

I got a job. My father told me that since he was now superintendent at the plant, he wanted to hire the best mechanic he knew. I accepted. Being back at something I understood was a good feeling. But if you think everything was perfect, you are wrong. Rudy and I still got the occasional sideways glance. No one seemed to want to carry that too far, though. I worked at the plant for several years, and since the pay wasn't bad, I didn't think about doing anything else.

Rudy graduated and, believe it or not, invited me to the senior prom that year. The superintendent that threw me out of school was gone. I still didn't know why, and I was not going to ask. Mr. James took his place. He said I could escort Rudy, but if I didn't act right, he would throw me out personally. Then he laughed again. Mr. James sure thought that anything I did was funny.

I felt out of place at a school social function, but it was fun, and everyone treated me with courtesy. That was more than I expected.

After graduation, Rudy went to the University of Arkansas, where her father graduated. She had always wanted to be a teacher, and that's what she is. Mr. James gave her a recommendation, and the school board hired her right back in the same school where she had grown up.

The Darmon brothers work at the bank. Brent and I thought this was funny until we realized that

RUDY AND JOEY: ORDINARY CHILDREN IN AN EXTRAORDINARY TIME

Julian Darmon's father had made the best business decision of his life. These two made more money as loan officers for that bank than can be imagined. Not only were they efficient; most people just couldn't stand to offend them. Those two are just good people and good businessmen. My father said that if Mr. Darmon would retire, the brothers would double the size of the bank in less than a year.

Brent is an insurance agent there. He said to me the other night that a good bullet wound is not such a bad thing, because his caused him to go into the insurance business. This was easy money according to Brent. I thought he worked sixteen hours a day, as we couldn't go anywhere without someone wanting to talk about policies or losses. Brent seemed to enjoy it.

I finally made good at the engine plant. I get to work in the performance shop, building high-performance engines for NASCAR drivers. It gets me a lot of attention that I don't need.

Sometimes I have to go to one of the speedways for testing. It's fun for a while, but I get homesick easy.

Just yesterday, after I had clocked out for the day, Rudy came to pick me up. I always enjoy Rudy picking me up. I can't explain why. I just like it. I was waiting with some men I didn't really know. When she drove up in blue jeans, a yellow shirt, and a yellow eye patch, one of the men said, "That your girlfriend?"

I'm J. B. Hood, remember?

I glared at him and retorted sharply, "No, that's my wife!"

ABOUT THE AUTHOR

The author is just a simple old man who lives in Oklahoma—a veteran and a confirmed believer in this amalgamated society. He has done so many things in his life, yet none are all that exciting or wonderful. He hopes these simple stories will catch your imagination and serve to remind you that good, no, *great* people of all races live and love everywhere in this magnificent country. Each one has a different outlook on life and, like the author, may take some thought to understand.

I offer these hopes for you. May the love of your life hold your hand and be continually close. May your family always be your supporters no matter what you choose for your life. Finally and most importantly, may God bless you continually in your search for love and success.